The Bake Shop Ghost

By **Jacqueline K. Ogburn**

Illustrated by **Marjorie Priceman**

Houghton Mifflin Company
Boston 2005

To all my friends who feed me, body and soul
—J.K.O.

To Uncle Bill
—M.P.

Text copyright © 2005 by Jacqueline K. Ogburn
Illustrations copyright © 2005 by Marjorie Priceman

www.houghtonmifflinbooks.com

The text of this book is set in Filosofia.

Library of Congress Cataloging-in-Publication Data
Ogburn, Jacqueline K.
The bake shop ghost / by Jacqueline K. Ogburn ; illustrated by Marjorie Priceman.
p. cm.
Summary: Miss Cora Lee Merriweather haunts her bake shop after her death,
until the new shop owner makes a deal with her.
ISBN 0-618-44557-9
[1. Ghosts—Fiction. 2. Cake—Fiction. 3. Bakers and bakeries—Fiction.] I.
Priceman, Marjorie, ill. II. Title.
PZ7.O3317Bak 2005
[E]—dc22
2004013186

ISBN-13: 978-0618-44557-8

Manufactured in China
SCP 10 9 8 7 6 5 4 3 2 1

Miss Cora Lee Merriweather ran the best bake shop in these parts—maybe even in the whole state. The chocolate in her Mississippi mud pie was darker than the devil's own heart. Her sponge cake was so light the angels kept hoping it would float up to heaven. No birthday was complete without a Merriweather layer cake with her special buttercream frosting.

Cora Lee must have poured all her sweetness into her work, because there wasn't much sweet about her looks. She had a lemon-pucker mouth and hair scraped back into a hard little bun.

Most folks hardly noticed her looks, though. She was seldom seen anywhere except behind the bake shop counter. Few looked up from the glass-fronted cases filled with fluffy meringue pies, glistening fruit tarts, flaky strudels, and, most of all, cakes. Layer cakes, sheet cakes, cakes with glazes, cakes with fillings, cakes with frosting finer than Irish lace, chocolate cakes, white cakes, tiny petits fours and towering wedding cakes.

When Cora Lee died, the whole town turned out for the funeral. No one cried until the preacher read out the bake shop menu and everyone realized that all those luscious desserts were now only sweet memories.

Cora Lee didn't have any family, so the Merriweather Bake Shop was sold.

*G*erda Stein was the first buyer. She made fine strudel and good cakes, although not quite up to Merriweather standards. A baker's day begins soon after midnight so that the cases are filled with fresh goods when the shop opens. Her first night in the shop, Gerda had trouble with the ovens — everything came out scorched. "Ah, these old ovens are as cranky as Cora Lee," Gerda muttered.

The next night, the refrigerator was broken. The milk and butter had spoiled. Gerda was scrubbing up the mess when she heard footsteps in the upstairs apartment where Cora Lee used to live. She listened nervously for a moment, but the footsteps stopped, so she went back to her cleaning.

Something clanked behind her. Slowly, Gerda turned around. A misty figure with hair pulled back in a hard little bun glared at Gerda, then shrieked, "Get out of my kitchen!" Gerda got.

The For Sale sign was back in the window that afternoon. "Cora Lee Merriweather is haunting this place," Gerda told everyone.

*F*rederico Spinelli bought the shop next. "No such things as ghosts," he said. "Besides, what ghost could resist my cannolis, my rum cake, my sweet chocolate éclairs?"

The next morning, Frederico looked like a ghost himself as he staggered out the front door. He was drenched in confectioners' sugar like a giant powdered doughnut.

$\mathcal{S}$ ophie Kristoff thought the shop was perfect for creating her cakes topped with marzipan decorations. Fruits, flowers, and small animals molded out of the dyed almond paste were her claim to fame. At sunrise, Sophie burst out the door, splattered with egg yolk and shells. Three pink marzipan pigs and a bunch of marzipan grapes came flying out right behind her.

After that, the Merriweather Bake Shop stood empty. The "M" and the "B" of the gold leaf lettering in the window flaked off. The shelves grew gray with dust. Years passed.

A nnie Washington had been the
pastry chef on a cruise ship.
She fell in love with the shop the
minute she stepped in the door. "Just
what I want — a kitchen that doesn't
rock up and down." She even liked the
apartment upstairs.

"A bucket of bleach, some cans of
paint, and I'll have this place shipshape in
no time," Annie said. She scrubbed and
polished, washed and waxed, primed and
painted. The ovens gleamed and the cases
sparkled. She unpacked her equipment, her
mixing bowls, cake molds, and recipe books.

That night, Annie hummed as she assembled the ingredients for a batch of puff pastry. About midnight, footsteps creaked overhead, but Annie paid no attention. A cold wind swept the room, but Annie kept working her dough.

A stack of mixing bowls went crashing to the floor.

Annie dusted off her hands and turned around. A tall white figure with a lemon-pucker mouth stood next to the worktable.

Annie smiled. "Miss Cora Lee Merriweather, I've been expecting you."

Cora Lee frowned. "Get out of my kitchen!"

Annie crossed her arms. "This is my kitchen now," she announced. Hovering utensils whirled through the air to crash into the wall. Annie didn't flinch. "I've been told you were the best baker ever in this town, maybe even in the state," she said. "Now, let me tell you something. I was the best pastry chef to ever sail on the Sea Star cruise ships. No typhoon, tsunami, or shipwreck ever stopped me from baking, and I never leave a kitchen until I'm done." She turned her back on the astonished ghost.

Cora Lee wasn't flummoxed for long. She let out a shriek that cracked the windowpane. Annie kept on rolling out her dough.

Cora Lee rose up through the counter into the middle of the puff pastry, making a most horrible face. Annie slapped a slab of butter on top of the pastry and folded it up, ghost and all.

Cora Lee began breaking eggs, a dozen at a time. Grim-faced, Annie scrubbed them up.

The battle went on all night, neither baker giving an inch.

At the crack of dawn, Cora Lee clawed open a fifty-pound bag
of flour, creating a blizzard that gave them both sneezing fits.

"Enough!" Annie cried. "What do you want? What can I do so you'll let me work in peace?"

Cora Lee stared through the swirling flour, then smiled a tight little smile. "Make me a cake," she said. "Make me a cake so rich and so sweet, it will fill me up and bring tears to my eyes. A cake like one I might have baked, but that no one ever made for me."

"Then you'll leave me to my work—no more pranks?" said Annie.

"The kitchen will be yours," Cora Lee agreed.

"Piece of cake," Annie said.

At the stroke of midnight, Cora Lee appeared in the kitchen. For the first time in years, the shop was buttery and warm with the scent of fresh baking. "Please, be my guest," Annie said, motioning to a place setting of fine china and silver. Cora Lee sat, shook out the linen napkin, and placed it in her lap.

Annie uncovered the first offering: a tiramisu covered with whipped cream and sprinkled with cocoa. She carefully cut a slice, adding a sprig of mint on the side.

Cora gave a small nod of approval and took a small bite. "Hmm—the cheese is a bit bland," the ghost said. Annie took a small slice for herself as Cora Lee finished off the cake. Annie decided Cora Lee was right about the cheese.

"I'll bet you've never had a moon cake before," Annie said as she lifted the next cover. "An entire Chinese Olympic diving team cried when they tasted this cake. It's made with red bean paste."

Cora Lee took a half-moon bite. "Can't say that I've ever tasted one before, but this doesn't bring tears to my eyes." Still, she ate the rest.

Annie presented cake after cake, and Cora Lee devoured them all. She showed no sign of being full, and her eyes hardly blinked, much less shed a tear. At sunrise, Cora Lee said, "You're a good baker, Miss Washington. But I'll not leave until you've baked me a cake to fill me up and bring tears to my eyes, a cake like one that I might have baked but that no one ever made for me."

And so it went. Annie made every kind of cake she knew. She made white cake, chocolate cake, fruit cake, spice cake, cheesecake, carrot cake, cake with nuts, cake with candy, cake from Asia, cake from Argentina, cakes from Vienna, Paris, and Rome. She made tortes and tarts, babkas and bundts, pound cake and *panforte*.

Each time, Cora Lee would sample the offering and remark on its quality before finishing it. Annie came to respect the ghost's judgment. Sometimes Cora Lee would help out a bit as Annie worked. Still, Annie began to fear that she would be stuck forever making cakes for the hungry ghost.

After a month and hundreds of cakes, Annie had run out of recipes. She went to the library, looking for inspiration. In a slim volume of town history, she found a section on Cora Lee and the Merriweather Bake Shop. When she had finished reading, she knew *exactly* what kind of cake to bake.

At midnight, as she had for the past month, Cora Lee appeared in the kitchen. Her place was set with china and silver. But there was just one covered cake on the counter. "Well, have you made me my cake?" asked Cora Lee.

"Yes, Miss Merriweather, I believe I have," Annie replied.

She lifted up the cover and tilted the cake toward the ghost. Across the top, in piped icing, it read, "Happy Birthday, Cora Lee."

The ghost looked up at Annie, her eyes brimming. "How did you know?"

"I found out that today is your one hundredth birthday and you grew up an orphan," said Annie. "Besides, who ever makes cake for the baker?" With her finest knife, Annie cut a slice of the chocolate layer cake with buttercream frosting and served it to Cora Lee.

Cora Lee ate her slice, tears trickling down her cheeks. When Annie offered her another, the ghost said, "I do believe I'm full." The two bakers sat quietly for a moment.

Cora Lee rose into the air. "It's your kitchen now. I'll keep our bargain and leave you in peace."

"Wait," said Annie, "I'd like to show you the new menu." She handed Cora Lee a menu card. The top line read, "Washington and Merriweather Bake Shop." Cora Lee's lemon-pucker mouth broke into a huge smile.

"What do you say?" asked Annie.

"Humph," said Cora Lee. "Since I'm the senior partner, it should be 'Merriweather and Washington.'"

"Oh, no—it's my kitchen now, you sly old ghost," said Annie.

Now the Washington and Merriweather Bake Shop is busier than ever. The old folks say the cakes are almost as good as Cora Lee's. Of course, they don't know she still bakes many of them. And every year, the shop's finest, most luscious, most beautiful birthday cakes are the ones that Cora Lee and Annie bake for each other.

Ghost-Pleasing Chocolate Cake

*T*his rich chocolate layer cake would satisfy the hungriest ghost. It is adapted by my friend Luli Gray, a wonderful writer and baker, from a recipe published in *Cook's Illustrated* magazine. Preheat your oven to 325 degrees. Prepare two 8- or 9-inch round pans or one 13-x-9-inch pan, by lining the bottoms with parchment or waxed paper or greasing the whole pan and dusting with flour. I recommend using the paper, as with this method the bottoms come out nice and smooth.

In a large bowl, mix together:

1½ cups sugar

1¼ cups all-purpose flour, sifted before measuring

¾ cup unsweetened cocoa

4 tablespoons buttermilk powder (available in supermarket baking sections)

½ teaspoon baking soda

¼ teaspoon salt

In a medium saucepan, melt over low heat:

1½ sticks unsalted butter

8 ounces bittersweet or semisweet chocolate

Remove from heat and add:

1 cup water

4 beaten eggs

1 teaspoon vanilla

Whisk the wet ingredients into the dry ingredients just until blended. Pour evenly into prepared pans, and bake on the middle rack of the oven about 35 to 40 minutes, or until a toothpick inserted into the middle of cake comes out with moist crumbs adhering to it. Do not overbake.

Cool thoroughly on a rack before icing.

Easy Frosting

This frosting can also be tinted with food coloring for decoration or writing.

3 cups confectioners' sugar

⅓ cup softened unsalted butter or shortening

¼ cup water

1 teaspoon vanilla extract

Pinch salt

Combine all ingredients in a large bowl and beat until smooth. If using an electric mixer, beat at low speed. Add more sugar for stiffer frosting.